NOT IN HERE,
DAD!

A Red Fox Book

Published by Random House Children's Books
20 Vauxhall Bridge Road, London SW1V 2SA

A division of Random House UK Ltd
London Melbourne Sydney Auckland
Johannesburg and agencies throughout the world

First published by Hutchinson Children's Books 1989
Red Fox edition 1990

Text © Cheryl Dutton 1989
Illustrations © Wendy Smith 1989

Printed in Singapore

NOT IN HERE, DAD!

DAD!

CHERYL DUTTON
Illustrated by Wendy Smith

RED FOX

Mr and Mrs Smith lived in a medium house with a medium garden.
They had a medium car, three medium children,
two goldfish and a hamster.
Mr Smith wasn't very fit. If he had to run for a bus,
he usually missed it.

At the school sports day,
he always came last in the Dads' race.

Even a meal out was a lonely business for poor old Dad.

At night things were even worse.
Dad kept everyone awake.
All because Dad . . .

SMOKED!

When Mr Smith went into the kitchen,
Mrs Smith shouted . . .

'NOT IN HERE, DAD!'

When Dad went into Peter's room, Peter cried . . .
'NOT IN HERE, DAD!'

When Dad went into Georgina's room, Georgina moaned . . .

'NOT IN HERE, DAD!'

Jamie just looked at Dad and said . . .

'YUK!'

And in the lounge, even the goldfish and the hamster squeaked . . .

'NOT IN HERE!'

So Dad hid in the bathroom and smoked and smoked and smoked.
The flowers on the wall gradually turned yellow.
Just like Dad's . . .

TEETH!

Dad found it difficult to breathe, so he went outside,
where the night was black. Just like Dad's . . .

LUNGS!

While Dad was out, Mrs Smith and the children sprayed
all over the house with air freshener because it . . .

STANK!
Just like Dad.

Finally there was only one place left for Dad to go — the garden shed.
But even the tools and the bikes and the lawnmower sighed . . .

'NOT IN HERE, DAD!'

Dad was fed up. All he wanted was some peace and quiet, so he decided to stop smoking.

Instead, he bit his nails and got very cross, he chewed gum
and had tantrums,

he ate sweets . . . and he cheated.

But eventually Dad stopped!

And if ever visitors dared to take out a cigarette, Dad
was the first to bellow . . .

'NOT IN HERE!'